Little Boys & Girls

Cover illustration by JON GOODELL

Illustrations by
KRISTA BRAUCKMANN-TOWNS
JANE CHAMBLESS WRIGHT
DREW-BROOK-CORMACK ASSOCIATES
KATE STURMAN GORMAN
JUDITH DUFOUR LOVE
BEN MAHAN
ANASTASIA MITCHELL
ANITA NELSON
ROSARIO VALDERRAMA

Louis Weber, C.E.O.
Publications International, Ltd.
7373 North Cicero Avenue
Lincolnwood, Illinois 60646

Manufactured in U.S.A.

8 7 6 5 4 3 2 1

ISBN: 0-7853-1649-3

PUBLICATIONS INTERNATIONAL, LTD.

Rainbow Books is a trademark of Publications International, Ltd.

Little Jack Horner

Little Jack Horner
  Sat in a corner
Eating his Christmas pie;

He put in his thumb,
  And pulled out a plum,
And cried, "What a good boy am I!"

Blue Bell Boy

I had a little boy,
    And called him Blue Bell;
Gave him a little work,
    He did it very well.

I made him go upstairs
    To bring me a gold pin;
In a coal bucket fell he,
    Up to his little chin.

Freddie and the Cherry Tree

Freddie saw some fine ripe cherries
    Hanging on a cherry tree.
And he said, "You pretty cherries,
    Will you not come down to me?"

"Thank you kindly," said a cherry,
    "We would rather stay up here;
If we ventured down this morning,
    You would eat us up, I fear."

Dirty Jim

There was one little Jim,
   'Tis reported of him,
And must be to his lasting disgrace,
   That he never was seen
With hands at all clean,
   Nor yet ever clean was his face.

His friends were much hurt
   To see so much dirt,
And often they made him quite clean;
   But all was in vain,
He got dirty again,
   And not at all fit to be seen.

My Little Brother

Little brother, darling boy
   You are very dear to me!
I am happy—full of joy,
   When your smiling face I see.

Shake your rattle—here it is—
   Listen to its merry noise;
And, when you are tired of this,
   I will bring you other toys.

My Little Sister

I have a little sister,
    She is only two years old;
But to us at home who love her,
    She is worth her weight in gold.

I must not taunt or tease her,
    Or ever angry be
With the darling little sister
    That God has given to me.

There Was a Little Girl

There was a little girl, who had a little curl,
    Right in the middle of her forehead,
And when she was good, she was very, very good.
    But when she was bad, she was horrid.

She stood on her head, on her little trundle bed,
    With no one there to say "no,"
She screamed and she squalled, she yelled and she bawled,
    And drummed her little heels against the window.

Her mother heard the noise, and thought it was the toys,
    Falling in the dusty attic,
She rushed up the flight, and saw she was alright,
    And hugged her most emphatic.

Little Polly Flinders

Little Polly Flinders
    Sat among the cinders
Warming her pretty little toes;
    Her mother came and stopped her,
For fear her lovely daughter
    Would toast her pretty little nose.

Little Fred

When Little Fred went to bed,
  He always said his prayers;
He kissed his mama, and then papa,
  And straightaway went upstairs.

My Little Maid

High diddle doubt, my candle's out
My little maid is not at home;
Saddle my hog and bridle my dog,
And fetch my little maid home.

Jack Jelf

Little Jack Jelf
   Was put upon a shelf
Because he could not spell "pie,"
   When his aunt, Mrs. Grace,
Saw his sorrowful face,
   She could not help saying, "Oh, my!"

And since Master Jelf
   Was put upon the shelf
Because he could not spell "pie,"
   Let him stand there so grim,
And no more about him,
   For I wish him a very good-bye!

Patience Is a Virtue

Patience is a virtue,
Virtue is a grace,
Grace is a little girl
Who wouldn't wash her face.